STITCH HEAD

The Pirate's Eye

Guy Bass

Illustrated by Pete Williamson

STRIPES

Foreword to the Past

(in the form of a rousing olde sea shanty sung by salty sea dogs)

When the seas be rough and the waves be quick —
Yo ho ho and slap your thigh! —
There's only one sailor who isn't sick,
Ahoy! Captain Flashpowder!

The waves do crash with brutish clout —
Yo ho ho and spit in your eye! —
But steady sails the Gadabout,
Ahoy! Captain Flashpowder!

The captain hunts for long-lost gold —
Yo ho ho and tickle your toes!
He'll be rich afore he's old,
Ahoy! Captain Flashpowder!

His eagle eye looks out to sea —
Yo ho ho and pick your nose!
He goes o'er the edge if he wants a wee,
Ahoy! Captain Flashpowder!

WELCOME TO
GRUBBERS
NUBBIN
(POPULATION 665)

Yesteryear

ALMOST-LIFE AND TIMES

(The Shadow of Castle Grotteskew)

"Onward, to Adventure!
Via Excitement!"

From
The Daring Diary of
Captain Flashpowder

Yesteryear! What a wonderful time it was. Yesteryear was filled with song and cheer, with funny hats and moustaches and horses pulling carts, with cobbled streets and expressions like "Lawks-a-mussy!" and "Hooken-snivey!". Yes, all in all, yesteryear was just about the most charming time to be alive.

Unless you lived in the small town of Grubbers Nubbin, that is. For in Grubbers Nubbin, even on the brightest day, a dark shadow fell upon the town. The shadow of

CASTLE GROTTESKEW.

High on a hill above the town loomed the castle. It had loomed there since before anyone could remember. The castle was home to the maddest of mad professors, Mad Professor Erasmus. For more years than it is possible to count on four people's fingers, the professor had busied himself creating hundreds of monstrous, unearthly creatures.

The very first of his creations was a small, almost-human creature that the professor had named **STITCH HEAd**.

Stitch Head was a jigsaw of bits, pieces and spare parts. His bald, round head was covered with stitches, and his eyes were different colours and sizes. One was black and forgettable, but the other was a bright, ice-blue orb that shimmered like the ocean on a cloudless morning.

Long since forgotten by his master, Stitch Head spent his days hiding in the darkest shadows of the castle, silently watching over the professor and his many creations. Fortunately, the castle's inhabitants rarely caused trouble. After all, they were some of the nicest unnatural horrors you were ever likely to meet.

But they hardly ever started out that way.

THE FIRST CHAPTER

THE ROOT OF ALL EVIL

(We're going to need a bigger dose)

> *"You haven't seen the world until you've seen it through a pirate's eye."*
>
> From
> *The Daring Diary of*
> *Captain Flashpowder*

"RUN!"

Stitch Head raced down the moonlit corridor, his mismatched eyes flashing with fear. He had a small bag slung over his shoulder, which clanked and clinked as he ran. In his tiny hand he gripped an ink-blue bottle.

"Empty…" he whispered – and looked behind him.

"Oh … oh no. It's here!"

A strange-looking, three-armed creature appeared from the gloom, stampeding after him. It was a hulking, beastly thing with a terrifying combination of monstrously abnormal parts. It charged along the corridor, gaining on Stitch Head with every step. Then, when it was almost upon him, its ear-piercing roar filled the air…

"WAAA-AAAHH! Faster, Stitch Head! It's going to EAT us to PIECES!" cried the Creature. Stitch Head and the Creature both glanced back. Behind them, in the dim light of the corridor, emerged *another* monster. It was huge – five times bigger than the Creature, and an impossible combination of octopus, sea snake, squid and upside-down-faced horribleness. It writhed its way towards them, roaring and screeching so loudly that it cracked the castle walls.

"GRREAAEOOORRGH!"

"I thought your POTION was meant to CURE it of its monstrousness!" cried the Creature (who, as it still hadn't fixed upon a name for itself, was just called the Creature).

"It was!" cried Stitch Head, searching in his potion bag as he tore down the corridor. "We're going to need a bigger dose!"

"WHAT do you think it's so GRUMPY about, anyway? It's only been almost-alive for FIVE MINUTES..." cried the Creature. "Maybe it didn't WANT to be brought to almost-life..."

"It's the *Root of All Evil!*" panted Stitch Head, as the shadow of the octo-monster loomed over them. "The professor's been growing the root in his laboratory ... he must have added it to his creation! It's made it ... *bad*. I thought my *Serenity Salve* would cure it but—"

"GRREEEOOOORRRGH!"

The tentacled octo-monster launched itself towards them with all its mad might. Stitch Head and the Creature leaped aside as the beast crashed through the floor, plummeting to the level below.

The Creature dusted itself off and peered though the hole left by the octo-monster.

"Well, THAT was a stroke of LUCK," it said. A moment later, the remainder of the ancient floor crumbled beneath their feet. Stitch Head and the Creature plunged to the lower level with an "*AAAAH!*" and a cascade of rubble.

ENTER ARABELLA

(A brand-new pair of kicking boots)

> *"Free treasure!*
> *What a steal!"*
>
> From
> *The Daring Diary of*
> *Captain Flashpowder*

"Creature?" whimpered Stitch Head, dragging himself to his feet. He looked around, but all he could see was rubble. Where was it? "Creature? Are you—"

A vast, dark shadow fell over Stitch Head. He heard a deep, rumbling growl and felt hot breath on the back of his head.

"Uh-oh…" he said in a tiny, imperilled whisper. He turned slowly to see the octo-monster looming over him.

"GREOOORGH!"

The octo-monster roared in Stitch Head's face, almost knocking him over with the force and foulness of its breath. Stitch Head stared into the beast's mouth, frozen with fear. This was the end. Silvery drool dripped like treacle from the octo-monster's hundred-toothed jaws as it closed in…

"Oi! Snot-breath! Don't make me come down there and smash your nose off!" came a cry. The octo-monster whirled round and looked up at the hole in the ceiling. There, standing on the edge, was a thin, scruffy-looking girl.

"Arabella…" whispered Stitch Head, peering up.

Arabella was a girl from Grubbers Nubbin and, apart from the professor, was the only human being Stitch Head could call a friend. Unlike the other townsfolk, Arabella couldn't get enough of the monsters, creatures and mad things in Castle Grotteskew. In fact, Stitch Head was pretty sure she wasn't scared of anything.

Even if she was about to be eaten.

"Arabella, get out of here!" shouted Stitch Head. "RUN!"

"GREOOOOOAAAEEGH!"

The octo-monster reared up to its full height, its tentacles flailing madly. But Arabella didn't budge. She just shook her head and pointed to her shoes.

"You see these?" said Arabella. "These are my brand-new kicking boots. They're polished up all nice and gleamy, so you'll be able to see your face in 'em when I kick it in..."

The octo-monster slithered up the wall and propelled itself through the hole with another rage-filled scream.

"ARABELLA! Hang on!" screamed Stitch Head, as the octo-monster wrapped one of its tentacles around Arabella and held her over the hole.

"I'll kick you into next week!" she growled, as the octo-monster gnashed its jaws...

"GREOO…ooR…GReorhh…uhhh…?"

Suddenly, the octo-monster shook its head and rubbed its huge, black eyes with two of its tentacles.

"My dear child, I must apologize unreservedly for such improper behaviour," it said – in a soft, eerily polite tone. "I cannot for the almost-life of me imagine what could have prompted such abominable conduct! Although I confess I don't remember anything at all... Even my own *name*. I simply *must* choose one — being nameless feels quite unseemly."

"TELL me about it," sighed the Creature.

"The *Serenity Salve*," whispered Stitch Head. "It's working..."

"Yeah, well, count yourself lucky," huffed a disappointed Arabella. "I was just about to get kicky all over your *face*."

"Then I am profoundly grateful I came to my senses when I did," said the octo-monster, lowering Arabella through the hole and placing her delicately on the ground.

"Now, if you'll be kind enough to allow me to take my leave, I suddenly feel rather dehydrated," continued the octo-monster. "Is there perchance a body of water in which I might take up residence?"

"There's … uh, there's a *moat* round the castle," said Stitch Head. "You can get to it via the sewer pipes — if you can squeeze through them…"

"A capital suggestion! My humblest thanks," said the octo-monster. "And if I can ever be of assistance — anything at all — just give me a whistle!"

With that, the giant octo-monster slid into the shadows of Castle Grotteskew.

"I don't even know if I *can* whistle…" muttered Stitch Head.

"Shame I scared him off," grumbled Arabella. "Would've been nice to try out my new boots…"

"Uh, I think it was the *Serenity Sal*— Never mind," said Stitch Head quietly. "Thanks for … wait, where's the Creature? Creature! Creature, answer me! Are you—?"

"That was GREAT!" boomed the Creature, clambering out from under a mound of rubble. "I haven't FALLEN through a HOLE on to my HEAD in WEEKS. It really clears out the COBWEBS. Hi, Arabella! I like your BOOTS! But HOW did you get into the CASTLE?"

"Got my own key made," replied Arabella, showing off a large key round her neck. "Good job too, that thing was going to swallow Stitch Head like a pickled egg. So, you thought of a name for yourself yet?"

"I've narrowed it DOWN," boomed the Creature excitedly. "Do you want to hear the SHORTLIST? I'll start with the As... ABRAHAM, ALBATROSS, ALBERT, ALFRED, ALGERNON, ALVIN, ANGELA, ANGELINA, ANGELO, ANTELOPE, ARCHIBALD, ARTHUR—"

"Blimey, Creature, I'll be older than my nan by the time you get to the Zs – and my nan's so ancient her toenails have fallen off!" chuckled Arabella.

"Hey, where ARE we?" asked the Creature, glancing around. "THIS doesn't look ANYTHING like the rest of the castle..."

Stitch Head cast his mismatched eyes across the room ... and froze.

"It can't be..."

"You all right?" asked Arabella. Stitch Head didn't reply. He just stared into the doorway. Arabella waved her hand in front of Stitch Head's face. "Anyone in there? You look like you've seen a ghost."

"I didn't think there WERE any GHOSTS in Castle Grotteskew..." said the Creature, panicking. "Should we start RUNNING and SCREAMING?"

"This is the room," whispered Stitch Head, finally.

"What room?" asked Arabella. "What is this place?"

"This is my master's – the professor's – old playroom," said Stitch Head. "This is where I was *created*."

THE FORGOTTEN ROOM

(The Daring Diary of Captain Flashpowder)

> *"Tomorrow is just an adventure you haven't had yet."*
>
> From
> *The Daring Diary of
> Captain Flashpowder*

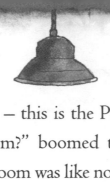

"NO WAY — this is the PROFESSOR's old playroom?" boomed the Creature. The Forgotten Room was like no other in the castle. It wasn't filled with brains in jars or hideous, half-finished creations. There were no chains hanging from the ceiling, or strange creations roaming about. Instead, there were playthings

— a rocking horse, a bucket of rusty tin soldiers, a moth-eaten teddy bear, a train set... And mountains of books, all covered in a thick layer of dust and cobwebs. In the middle of the room was the only clue to the professor's future — a small table attached to a makeshift electrical generator.

"You was born here?" asked Arabella.

"Well, *made...*" said Stitch Head.

"Of COURSE you're well made!" bellowed the Creature reassuringly. "The stitches really bring out the different bits of your FACE."

"That — that's a *creating table*. It's where my master brought me to almost-life," said Stitch Head, pointing to the table. "This room was my home for years. When my master's father took him away to become a mad professor, I was locked inside. I hoped my master would come back for me ... but he never did. Eventually, one of his mad monsters rampaged through the castle. It broke down the door and freed me. But by then the castle was full of creations, and I was *forgotten*."

"POOR Stitch Head," whimpered the

Creature, wiping away a tear with its third arm.

"You'd better not start crying," groaned Arabella. "*Crybabies* make me clench my fists."

"I-I wasn't GOING to…" replied the Creature with a sniff.

"You know what you need, Stitch Head?" said Arabella, as she started sifting through the piles of books. "You need to get *out* more."

"That's a GREAT idea!" cried the Creature, who thought almost everything was a great idea. "We should go on a TRIP! We could all go to the BEACH and work on our TANS. I'm such a PALE shade of GREY these days…"

"Leave Grotteskew? We can't! I mean I can't – not *ever*," said Stitch Head, with a rare firmness.

Only once had Stitch Head ventured

beyond the castle walls. One dark, foreboding night, a circus ringmaster by the name of Fulbert Freakfinder had come calling at Grotteskew's Great Door, promising Stitch Head fame and fortune as the star of his *Travelling Carnival of Unnatural Wonders*. For the first time, Stitch Head had considered the possibility that there was something more to almost-life than being forgotten. Indeed, but for Freakfinder's final betrayal, he might have left Castle Grotteskew for ever. What would have become of his master then? Who would have cured each new creation of its madness and monstrosity? Stitch Head never forgave himself for his selfishness. From that moment he vowed never to leave the castle again.

"I'm sorry, but I can't leave," Stitch Head repeated, wiping the dust from the professor's creating table. "The professor *needs* me."

"Yeah, right … needs you to cure all his mad monsters, you mean," tutted Arabella, as she tossed books over her shoulder. "I'm surprised he ain't better at it, what with all these professoring manuals — there's hundreds of 'em! He should get another hobby, or… Hang on, what's this?"

She picked up a thick, leather-bound book and blew off the dust. On the cover were the words:

"Who's Captain Flashpowder?" asked Arabella, holding up the book. Beneath the title was a painting of a heroic-looking, eye-patched figure. In his hand he wielded a gleaming cutlass. He was standing at the stern of a huge ship — a *pirate* ship — a bright red and yellow parrot perched on his shoulder.

"My master *loved* that book," whispered Stitch Head, his ice-blue eye gleaming in the moonlight. "He used to read it to me every night. It's the diary of a great pirate. It tells of his adventures to far-off lands, searching for treasure … excitement … piracy on the high seas."

"GREAT! I LOVE pirates!" the Creature exclaimed. "HEY, that gives me an IDEA — let's play PIRATES! Oh, can we, PLEASE? All the other creations want to play is TEA PARTIES…"

"Stitch Head will have to be Captain Flashpowder," said Arabella, showing the Creature the diary. "He's already got his eye. Look!"

"Hey, you're RIGHT!" boomed the Creature. "Captain FLUSHPOWDER's got Stitch Head's eye. I mean, Stitch Head's got HIS! I mean—"

"What . . . what do you mean?" asked Stitch Head. He peered at the diary's cover. Flashpowder's left eye was bright, piercing, almost glimmering – and ice blue.

Arabella chuckled. "Ain't no denying it, Stitch Head – that eye of yours is the absolute spit of the pirate's."

"Are . . . are my eyes different?" asked Stitch Head, a little embarrassed. He didn't make a habit of looking at his reflection. Seeing himself only reminded him how small and unimpressive he was compared to the other creations in the castle. He had no idea that one of his eyes looked different from the other.

"Stitch Head," said Arabella. "It's about time you had a good *look* at yourself."

UPON REFLECTION

(Stitch Head's eye)

> "Keep your eye on the horizon and your poop on the poop deck."

From
*The Daring Diary of
Captain Flashpowder*

Arabella took a small pocket mirror out of her dress.

"Is that so you can make sure you look NICE and PRETTY?" boomed the Creature.

"No, it's so I can see folk sneaking up on me," replied Arabella. "Boys like to pull my hair, and I like to smash their teeth out for trying."

"Now REMEMBER, Stitch Head," began the Creature. "There's no SHAME in SCREAMING at your HIDEOUSNESS. I do it ALL the time."

"Stop worrying. I've seen stray dogs uglier than you," said Arabella, holding out the mirror. "Here, have a butcher's."

Stitch Head peered into the mirror. He saw his round, worried face staring back at him. The first thing he noticed were his stitches, which ran like tiny train tracks across his face, separating the pale patches of skin.

"See? Not so bad, is it?" added Arabella.

Stitch Head shrugged. He didn't look as strange as most of the professor's creations ... and he certainly didn't feel like screaming. He peered closer. His right eye glinted hypnotically. It was bright, ice blue – and looked *exactly* like Captain Flashpowder's.

"SEE?" hollered the gleeful Creature. "You've got a PIRATE's EYE! You're part SWASHBUCKLER!"

"But that's not possible ... is it?" began Stitch Head. He knew he was made up from spare parts, but he'd never really thought about where they came from.

Stitch Head sat down on a pile of books.

"What does it mean?" he whispered.

"What do you think it means?" said Arabella. "It means the professor somehow got hold of Flashpowder's diary and his lost eye –

and he gave that eye to *you*. The Creature's right — you might look like a rag doll that's been run over by a horse … but you're part *pirate*."

<hr />

That night, with Arabella back home in Grubbers Nubbin and the Creature posing for an almost-life class with some of the other creations, Stitch Head made his way deep into the maze-like bowels of the castle, far from the Forgotten Room, down winding, unlit staircases until he reached the dankest, darkest corner of Castle Grotteskew — the dungeon that he called home.

There, he lay on his bed and opened *The Daring Diary of Captain Flashpowder*. It suddenly felt as if no time had passed since the professor had read it to him back in the playroom.

Zounds abounds!
Here be writ the most daring
exploits of I, Captain Dash
Flashpowder, the most undaunted
pirate ever to set sail upon the seas!

Together with my loyal crew and
trusty parrot companion, Pilgrim,
I journey the world aboard the good
ship Gadabout, in search of hidden
treasures, lost islands and voyages to...
The Edge of Possibility.

Zounds abounds!
Fix your eye on the horizon and
let's set sail.
Onward ... to adventure!

Stitch Head's mind was racing with possibilities. Could Flashpowder's lost eye really have found its way to Castle Grotteskew, along with his diary? He felt his almost-living heart beat ever faster as he turned the page.

Captain's chronicle, September the 25th
Day 313 aboard my trusty vessel, the Gadabout.

By my boots! My trusty queen and mistress, the Sea, is as choppy as if a giant squid were rocking the ship with its eight monstrous tentacles! Which is impossible, because I killed that squid last week! Zounds abounds! Flashpowder: 1, Squid: 0!
    But, while the smell of my trusty crew's seasickness grows stronger by

the day, so, too, does the smell of buried treasure! (Not literally. Treasure smells not.) For today, my trusty companion, Pilgrim, returned from his flight with gratifying news. He has found land! At least I think that's what he said. It was mainly squawking. Squawk! Squawk! Squawk! All day, every day…
One day I shall strangle that trusty companion.

Where was I? Oh, yea! Land! Land means treasure … treasure means danger … danger means adventure.

Avast ye! Hoist the mizzen mast! Splice the mainbrace! Swab the poop deck! By my lonely, gleaming eye, we sail once more to adventure!

"To adventure," repeated Stitch Head. He closed the book and looked again at the cover, staring into Flashpowder's eye. The resemblance to his own eye was uncanny. Could he really be part pirate? Stitch Head suddenly wondered if he was destined for more than just hiding away in a castle for the rest of his days. After all, shouldn't even a *part* pirate be out sailing the oceans, looking for lost islands and hidden treasure?

Stitch Head sighed, remembering his promise to his master. He could never leave Castle Grotteskew, not as long as Professor Erasmus called it home.

Still, that was all the more reason to dream. He tried to picture himself aboard the *Gadabout*, the sun warming his skin as he strode up and down the deck. He tried to picture the waves buffeting the ship as he cast his ice-blue eye out to the horizon, to a distant, treasure-filled island. He tried imagining his crew singing bold sea shanties as they swabbed the poop deck. He felt for the sword by his side and held out his arm for the return of his trusty companion.

But the more Stitch Head tried to picture himself as Captain Flashpowder, the more he was reminded of who he *really* was — a mad professor's small, forgotten creation.

No, if he was going to imagine himself as a pirate...

He had to *become* a pirate.

A TRUSTY SWORD

(Stitch Head looks for his inner pirate)

> *"Whoever said the pen is mightier than the sword has only ever been stabbed with a pen."*
>
> From
> *The Daring Diary of Captain Flashpowder*

Stitch Head spent the rest of the night making a list of all the really piratey things about Captain Flashpowder.

A trusty ship

A trusty crew

A trusty companion
(preferably a parrot)

A trusty sword

An ice-blue eye

"An ice-blue eye" didn't seem vital to becoming a pirate, but it was the one thing he and Flashpowder had in common. All the other stuff seemed quite hard to come by. Where on earth was he going to get a ship? Or a parrot, for that matter?

Stitch Head decided to start small. He found a slim piece of wood and whittled one end to a point with a not-particularly-sharp rock. Then he found a smaller piece of wood and tied it on near the base with a piece of rope.

"My trusty sword," he said. He gingerly began swinging the piece of wood, trying to imagine he was Captain Flashpowder facing off against a fearsome sea serpent or a horde of ghost-pirates. In the end, it just made him feel like a mad professor's first creation swinging a piece of wood. Determinedly, he clambered on to a nearby table and reached up for one of the many chains that hung from the ceiling. He grabbed the chain and leaped into the air, imagining he was swinging from the rigging of the *Gadabout*!

"A fast ye!" he cried in his loudest whisper, as he flew across the dungeon. "Spice the

mail brace! Hoist the
middle mast! To
adventuooOOOOH!"

KRUMP!

Stitch Head flew
face-first into a wall and
slid to the ground with a
FLUD.

"*Oww...*"

He lay motionless for a minute,
the sound of the chains still clanging in his
ears. Then he checked to see if any of his
stitches had come loose and inspected his
sword, which had snapped halfway down. He
took another piece of rope and tied it round
his waist like a belt. Then he hooked in the
sword ... and sighed. He still didn't feel like a
pirate – at *all*.

He needed a trusty companion.

A TRUSTY COMPANION

(Stitch Head visits the laboratory)

"A trusty companion should be brave, fearless, reliable ... and, in case of emergency, edible."

From
*The Daring Diary of
Captain Flashpowder*

At sunrise, Stitch Head set to work finding himself a trusty companion.

Of course, there was the Creature. It had been Stitch Head's "bestest friend" since the day of its creation, when Stitch Head had cured it of a nasty case of werewolfism. He trusted the Creature more than anyone, but he couldn't exactly keep it perched on his shoulder. No, Stitch Head needed a *parrot*.

His master, Professor Erasmus, had a baffling collection of "ingredients" for use in his experiments. His laboratory was filled with an extensive store of less-than-alive creatures (or parts of them) from all over the world. Surely he must have a parrot or two lying around?

Over the years, Stitch Head had found a dozen different ways of getting inside the laboratory – and all without being spotted by his master. Until now he had been looking for ingredients for his cures – the endless potions, tonics and ointments he'd created to stop his professor's more *unpredictable* creations from running wild. But today, only a parrot would do.

Stitch Head crawled through a crack in the east wall of the laboratory. It was a huge, high-ceilinged room, with plenty of dark shadows in which to hide – even as the light of the morning tried to creep in.

At the far end of the laboratory, the professor was pacing up and down near his desk. He was clutching a handful of notes and calculations and mumbling things like, "AHAH! It must have bigger toes!" and "How many brains are too many?"

Stitch Head made for the other end of the room, where the professor kept his vast store of "ingredients". Along the far wall was a high, broad tower of wooden shelves, filled to bursting with crates, boxes and jars, each containing things of unimaginable strangeness – and labelled accordingly.

Stitch Head passed by a jar of eyes marked "SLIGHTLY ALIVE EYES – HANDLE WITH STARE". He instinctively looked away as the eyes bobbed about in the yellowy liquid.

"Cat's whiskers … dog breath … dragon's teeth…" he mumbled, as he moved along the first shelf – jar after jar, bottle after bottle. There was nothing that even resembled a parrot. He clambered up on to a higher shelf and began carefully making his way along it.

"Crow's feet … owl brains … elephant memory lobes…" he muttered, as he shuffled along the shelf. There was still no sign of even a piece of a parrot. He climbed higher.

By the time he had reached the highest shelf, Stitch Head had almost given up hope. The shelf itself was rotting and covered in cobwebs, and crammed with dozens of neglected, sorry-looking sacks marked "SPARE PARTS". These were the bits and pieces that simply weren't good enough for his master's impressive creations ... just like the parts the young professor had found to make Stitch Head, all those years ago.

But then, at the far end of the shelf, he spotted something glinting in the lamplight – a large, dust-covered jar, marked "PICKLED PARROT PARTS".

"*Perfect…*" whispered Stitch Head. "And perfectly *pickled*."

He made his way cautiously along the shelf, the ancient, dry wood splintering beneath him. He dared to look down and realized how perilously high he had climbed. He held his breath and fixed his gaze on the bright colours of the parrot parts. He reached out with his tiny arm, but it was too far away. He shuffled along a bit further … and heard a loud CREEEAAK.

"Uh-oh," Stitch Head muttered, as he felt the shelf start to buckle. He stared down in horror to see the wood splinter and crack … and the parrot jar begin to slide off the shelf! He grabbed it with both hands, but it was too heavy. For a moment, it was as if time stood still. Stitch Head held on for dear almost-life – and he, the jar and a dozen or so sacks of spare parts plummeted to the ground!

"AaaaaaAAAH—"

SKAAASH!

The jar shattered into a thousand shards, sending pieces of pickled parrot flying across the laboratory. Stitch Head panicked. The professor! What if he caught his first creation stealing from him?

Stitch Head scrambled to his feet, slipping and sliding in the slick of spilled pickling goo. Then, as he raced for the crack in the wall, he instinctively grabbed one of the strewn "spare parts" sacks. He had almost made his escape when he stopped … and looked back.

"I know! I'll add another head!" screamed the professor, oblivious to Stitch Head's mishap. "Mad professoring is all about extra heads, these days! This will be my greatest creation ever! AHAHA-AHAHAA!"

Stitch Head kicked himself for feeling nervous. He needn't have worried about his master noticing him – or the broken jar. All that concerned the professor was his next creation. He sighed, slung the sack over his shoulder and disappeared into the shadows.

STITCH HEAD'S FIRST CREATION

(Part monkey, part bat)

> *"Piracy is a point of view."*
>
> From
> *The Daring Diary of
> Captain Flashpowder*

Stitch Head made his way to the Forgotten Room. It was still early and the castle was quiet. The Creature (who was quite the social butterfly) was no doubt regaling the other creations with tails of their octo-monster escapade, so it was the perfect time to work without fear of interruption.

He emptied the "spare parts" sack on to the creating table. There was one mostly mouldy monkey and a few bits of battered bat … hardly the ideal ingredients for a trusty companion.

Stitch Head stared at the parts and began assembling them in his head. He had watched so many of his master's experiments brought to life, it almost seemed like second nature to him. He quickly set to work, toiling all day and all night on his creation.

By the following morning, his trusty

companion was ready to be brought to almost-life.

"Here goes nothing," he said to himself, looking down at the tiny, cobbled-together creature. Stitch Head pumped in the last of the cultivation goo, attached a handful of electrodes and turned on the makeshift generator. It hadn't been used for more than forty years – did it still work? Did it have enough power to bring the creation to almost-life, as it had him? There was only one way to find out…

"Live … *please*," he added, and pulled the life-lever. After a moment, bright blue bolts of electricity darted out of the machine and through the electrodes. The creature began to shake uncontrollably and grey smoke poured from its ears.

FTZZZZ-KRKLE-TZZZZZ!

"Uh, less power? More? What do I do?"
cried Stitch Head, his hand gripping the life-
lever. Suddenly, the generator began to spark
and fizz as if it were coming apart at the seams.
A barrage of loose nuts and bolts fired across
the room as the machine started glowing with
uncontrolled energy...

TZZ-KRKLE-TZZZZZ!

"Uh-oh," whimpered Stitch Head — and dived for cover.

KA-KOOOOOM!

The generator exploded! Stitch Head crashed head-first into a pile of books as shards of sparking metal flew past him! He scrambled to his feet and peered into the thick smoke. Had his creation been blown to bits? After a moment, he saw something *move*.

"H-hello?" he said. He waved the smoke away with his hands. There, on the floor, sat a small, blue-grey creature. He was a strange, unpleasant combination of parts. While he was more or less monkey-shaped, his front legs were the folded wings of a bat, along with his wide, flat nose and ears. The monkey-bat unfolded his wings as if he were trying to remember what they were.

"I-I *did* it. My first creation — my very own … monkey-bat! My trusty companion…" whispered Stitch Head. He knelt down and held out his hand. "It's OK, don't be afraid. I am Stitch Head. I'm your *master*."

The monkey-bat chirruped and cocked his head.

Then he bared his teeth and his eyes flooded with rage.

"GRrrrRRRR…"

"Uh-oh," said Stitch Head.

"GRRAAAAHH!"

I SHALL CALL HIM ... POX

(Arabella saves the day again)

"Just because I'm stealing from you, doesn't mean we can't be friends!"

From
*The Daring Diary of
Captain Flashpowder*

As it turned out, Stitch Head's first creation was also the most vicious, monstrous creature he had ever met – and that was saying something. After all but destroying the Forgotten Room, the tiny monkey-bat flew into the castle. Stitch Head barely escaped with his stitches intact. He hurried down to his dungeon home and gathered all the calming curatives, soothing salves and treating tonics he could cram into his bag.

As he raced out of the dungeon, the monkey-bat was already rampaging through the castle. Stitch Head simply followed the terrified screams of the castle's other creations to discover the whereabouts of his "trusty companion".

Before long, he found himself in the most populated part of the castle. Stitch Head rarely ventured this far. He had yet to introduce himself to the hundreds of Grotteskew's generally genial creations — motorized lizard-ladies, skull-faced brains, beetle-bodied bug-boys, steam-driven mechanopillars — because wherever he turned, he was reminded of his master's mad genius, and his own insignificance.

But today, he didn't have time to hide in the shadows. He raced between the creations' legs (and wheels and tentacles) as the mad monkey-bat flew from victim to victim.

"AAIEE! Oliver, save me!" screamed a two-tailed snake-man with robot arms, as the monkey-bat attacked. "It's eating my favourite end!"

"Mercy!" shrieked a tin-plated skeleton. "He wants to kill me! I can feel it in my bones!"

"Help! It's going for my phantom limb!" cried a bodiless head.

Even when Stitch Head managed to get close enough to administer a potion, the monkey-bat would simply sneeze and continue his rampage. If he made it to the professor's laboratory, who knew what might happen? Stitch Head had to do something.

He needed help.

"But I was JUST about to take a BATH..." groaned the Creature, as Stitch Head dragged it along the stone corridor towards the commotion-causing monkey-bat.

"He's destroying the castle!" cried Stitch Head. "We have to stop this ... thing before he does something *terrible*."

"So you REALLY made your very own CREATION?" asked the Creature. "Does that mean you're a MAD PROFESSOR now?"

"No ... no, of course not!" Stitch Head replied. "I was just ... trying something. But this thing is, well, he's *mad*."

"But NO ONE is better than YOU at making MAD things UN-MAD," said the Creature. "I mean, you CURED me of werewolfism TWICE! You're the BEST..."

"Not this time," Stitch Head replied. "I've created an *incurable* monster! I've made a—"

Stitch Head froze as he noticed sunlight streaming in from the open courtyard door. The monkey-bat was outside. If he flew over the castle walls...

Stitch Head and the Creature crept out into the courtyard. At the far end was the Great Door to the outside world – and in the centre, perched atop a statue of the professor, was the monkey-bat.

"RrRRrrr-AaaR! *SWARRTIKI!* GRUKK!" growled the monkey-bat, his eyes darting around for something to savage.

"Wait... THAT'S what you're so WORRIED about?" laughed the Creature. "THAT tiny little THINGY?"

"He's trying to escape the castle," said Stitch Head. "We can't let that happen..."

"Leave it to ME," said the Creature, striding towards the statue. "The IMPORTANT thing is to show this thingy who's BOSS…"

"Creature, wait!" cried Stitch Head … but it was too late. The Creature was already halfway across the courtyard.

"Now LOOK here, little thingy," began the Creature. "I know how HARD it is being brought to ALMOST-LIFE … everything seems so STRANGE and almost-new. But that's a PERFECTLY almost-natural feeling. There's nothing to FEAR. You're among BESTEST friends here!"

The monkey-bat stared at the Creature for a moment, his blood-red eyes all but glowing with feral rage.

"GrrRRRRRRR…"

"UH-oh," began the Creature. "Why is the thingy GROWLING at me?"

"GRAAAAHH!"

"Creature! Look out!" yelled Stitch Head as the monkey-bat swooped. He landed on the Creature's head and began biting and scratching with all his monstrous rage!

"AAHH! Get him OFF! He's making a MEAL of me!" squealed the Creature, flailing wildly as the monkey-bat ripped chunks of hair off its head with his teeth. "Why didn't you WARN me he was MONSTROUS?"

Stitch Head raced across the courtyard and scaled the Creature's coat until he reached its head. There, he came face to face with the monkey-bat.

"Uh… A fast ye…" he said, nervously drawing his broken sword.

"YaBBiT! GRRAAAAAHH!" shrieked the monkey-bat, preparing to pounce…

It was precisely then that Stitch Head heard the CLUNK-KRUNK of a key turning in the Great Door.

It was *opening!* But how? No one could open it except…

"Only me!" said a voice, as the Great Door

creaked open. "Blimey, this door's heavier than my old nan when I have to carry her to the toilet..."

"Arabella! No!" cried Stitch Head, but the monkey-bat had already spotted his escape route. As Arabella emerged from behind the door, Stitch Head's first creation took to the air, gliding straight towards her.

"Arabella, look OUT! He's HUNGRY for HAIR!" screamed the Creature, as the monkey-bat crashed into Arabella, sending them both barrelling across the courtyard.

"Arabella! No! Go, Creature, go!" shouted Stitch Head, hanging on to what was left of the Creature's hair. The Creature lumbered towards them, as Arabella and the monkey-bat rolled across the ground, kicking up clouds of dust. Arabella's pained screams filled the air ... or was it laughter?

"Ha ha! Finally, a mad thing that's actually got some get-up-and-gouge!" Arabella giggled, as the monkey-bat gnawed happily on her arm. "I was beginning to think there wasn't nothing in this castle with an ounce of backbone. He's great!"

"He – he is?" said Stitch Head.

"Sit, mad thing, sit!" The monkey-bat immediately flew into the air and landed obediently on Arabella's shoulder, like a parrot, except with more ear chewing. "He's a bit *tame* for my liking, but he'll do. Can I keep him?"

"Maybe your POTIONS have finally WORKED," mused the Creature. "Maybe he's CURED…"

"Maybe," replied Stitch Head. He leaped to the ground and tentatively held out a hand to the monkey-bat. The monkey-bat snarled – and immediately tried to bite it off. "Or maybe not," added Stitch Head.

"I've never had a pet before – not since that dead rabbit I found," said Arabella, stroking the monkey-bat behind his ears. "I shall call him … Pox, after the town's last plague."

"But…" began Stitch Head. Then he shrugged and smiled weakly. Arabella was clearly the only one who could tame the beast – perhaps he could live without a trusty companion. Pox hadn't exactly made him feel like a pirate, anyway. But what would?

"By the way," continued Arabella, "the postman handed me a letter. He was too chicken to come up to the castle himself, the big baby…"

"A LETTER? Ooh, I LOVE getting letters!" bellowed the Creature. "At least, I would if I ever DID."

"But we *never* get letters," said Stitch Head suspiciously.

Arabella took the letter out of her dress pocket and handed it to Stitch Head. He stared at the envelope. It was creased and crumpled, but with a fine, red-wax stamp sealing it down. Upon it was written:

To Be Delivered in Pressing Confidence
And With Utmost Care to
Professor Erasmus
Castle Grotteskew
Grubbers Nubbin

"It – it's for the professor…" said Stitch Head, a shiver running down his spine. Suddenly, thoughts of piracy on the high seas seemed very unimportant indeed. Stitch Head felt a strange sense of impending dread … as if the outside world was banging on the Great Door…

THE LETTER

(Stitch Head's special delivery)

*"You've been boarded by –
you've been robbed by –
a smooth criminal."*

From
*The Daring Diary of
Captain Flashpowder*

Despite the Creature's insistence that he should "TEAR open!" the letter, Stitch Head decided that whatever the letter contained his master should be the first to see it. He, the Creature and Arabella (accompanied by her new "pet", Pox the monkey-bat) made their way to the rafters above the professor's laboratory. It was Stitch Head's favourite place in the castle.

As ever, the professor was hard at work assembling an impressively mad creation. He'd laid out a bizarre assortment of components that he was ordering and reordering in a number of horrifying combinations.

"AhHaA! The knee bone connects to the ... snake head!" guffawed the professor. "The elbow connects to the bear claw! AHAHA!"

"Are you SURE you don't want a quick PEEK?" asked the Creature, as Stitch Head held the letter in his tiny hands. "What if it's IMPORTANT?"

"I read all my nan's secret letters," said Arabella. "Course, my nan can't actually write, so they don't make much sense…"

Stitch Head's fingers hovered over the wax seal.

"I-I can't," he said finally. "It's not for … *creation* eyes. It's for the professor."

He held the letter out in front of him … and dropped it. It fluttered gently through the air and landed on the laboratory table.

"The shin bone's connected to the … antlers! The wrist bone's connected to the … horse's hoof! AhAHaA!" cackled the professor. Then, "The thigh bone's connected to this … letter?"

"He's FOUND it! GREAT! Oh, this is SO EXCITING!" boomed the Creature.

"Shhhh...." said Stitch Head.

He watched his master tear open the letter and read it as if it was taking up valuable creating time. Finally, he tossed the letter to the floor.

"HUH..." began the Creature. "Maybe it wasn't so important AFTER—"

"AHAHAHAHAHAHAHAAAAA!" screeched the professor. Finally! After all these long, professoring years! I must pack! A-AHAHAHAaaAAAA!"

"Pack?" repeated Stitch Head. For the first time in his almost-life, Stitch Head watched the professor abandon his latest creation and race out of the laboratory.

"What was all that about?" asked Arabella. "He's *mad*, that mad professor of yours."

"YaBBit!" agreed Pox, through a mouthful of Arabella's hair.

"Forget what I said," said Stitch Head. "We *have* to read that letter."

After ten minutes of clambering (the Creature suddenly decided it was scared of heights), Stitch Head and his companions made it to the laboratory floor. Stitch Head found the letter in amongst a pile of skulls and picked it up. He took a deep breath and read it, his heart skipping more beats than usual.

To the Esteemed Creator of Monsters, Creatures and Mad Things

Professor Erasmus,

CONGRATULATIONS!

You have been awarded Mad Professoring's Most Genuine Honour,

The Lifetime of Mad Professoring Award!

The Guild of Mad Professors has chosen you to be our Exceptional Guest at a Most Proper Ceremony to be held in your honour.

Come to the Grand Olde Town of Oldetown,
A day's ride from Castle GrottesKew.

We look forward to greeting you at your earliest convenience.

Sincerely,

PROFESSOR

K. E. FARFRIEND,

DMP (Doctor of Mad Professoring)

"SO, what does it SAY?" asked the Creature.

"He *won*," muttered Stitch Head. "He won a mad professoring award. I didn't even know there *was* a mad professoring award. But he won. He won!"

Stitch Head felt happier than he had in years. His master's work had finally been recognized! "I always knew – I mean, I always hoped that ... no one can create like my master! He's the best there is…"

"Yeah, it's all very whoop-dee-doo an' lah-dee-dah," huffed Arabella, "but don't it mean that the professor is going to—"

SLAM!

The castle shook with the sound of the Great Door slamming shut.

"Go…" whispered Stitch Head.

As it turned out, the professor hadn't even

bothered to pack – he'd just left. For the first time in Stitch Head's almost-life, the castle was without its mad professor ... and he was without a master.

A TRUSTY SHIP

(Try to focus on the piracy)

> "*A pirate without a ship
> is like a port without
> a starboard!*"
>
> From
> *The Daring Diary of
> Captain Flashpowder*

Stitch Head had never imagined that the professor would – *could* – leave Castle Grotteskew. He'd never even known him to look out of the window. He was sure his master would return soon – nothing could keep him away from his work for long. But it left Stitch Head feeling strangely lost ... how should he spend his days if not looking out for his master?

He was still staring at the letter as he and his friends wandered through the dark stone corridors of the castle.

"I know! Let's pretend we're MAD PROFESSORS!" boomed the Creature "We can FILL in while he's AWAY!"

"Speaking of which," began Arabella, pointing to Pox as he flew alongside her. "The Creature told me Pox is *your* doing. Since when did you start creating creations?"

Stitch Head hung his head, suddenly embarrassed.

"I wasn't professoring," he replied, folding the professor's letter and tucking it into his sleeve. "I was … I was trying to make a trusty companion. I was trying to be like Captain Flashpowder."

"I knew it! Is that what that old bit of wood is on your belt?" Arabella laughed. "You're trying to be a pirate!"

"I was just trying to imagine it," mumbled Stitch Head, more ashamed than ever. "I made a list of *piratey* things. I just thought, because of the eye, maybe I could … I don't know. It's *stupid*."

"What are you TALKING about? That's a GREAT idea!" shrieked the Creature with glee. "We can finally pretend we're PIRATES! No more 'tea parties'!"

"Sounds good to me," said Arabella. "I ain't done no piracy since Travelling Aunt Olga took me on that cruise…"

"I don't know … I'm not sure I'm cut out for it," sighed Stitch Head. "Whatever I do, I can't imagine anything except these walls. I can't *see* myself as a pirate…"

"You just need to think BIGGER!" bellowed the Creature happily. "So, what ELSE is on that LIST of yours?"

Stitch Head didn't get far down his list – no sooner had he mentioned "a trusty ship" than the Creature squealed with excitement, and jumped up and down with such enthusiasm that the ground shook.

"A SHIP! That's PERFECT! We'll BUILD our own PIRATE SHIP! Nothing says 'Look at how PIRATEY I am!' like a nice, big SHIP."

"But how?" asked Stitch Head. "We'd need materials – timber, iron, cloth for the sails…"

"You ain't *never* going to discover your inner pirate if you don't have a bit of faith," huffed Arabella. "That prof of yours is away for a day or two at least, so we've got the run of the place – a castle to plunder! He won't notice a few things gone missing – he never goes nowhere except that lab of his, anyway."

"I-I…" began Stitch Head. He didn't like the idea of pilfering from the castle, despite the fact he'd been "stealing" from the professor for years to make his cures. Then again, building a ship would be a nice distraction while the professor was away … and he *did* long to discover his inner pirate. He took a deep breath.

"Let's do it."

SHIP SHAPE

(Building the *Gadabout II*)

"The trouble with eyepatches is no one knows whether you're blinking or winking."

From
*The Daring Diary of
Captain Flashpowder*

Arabella was quick to come up with a strategy for building Stitch Head's pirate ship. They would work in the courtyard, so they had plenty of space for all the masts, jibs, bowsprits and topsails. Stitch Head would design it, based on the drawings of the *Gadabout* in *The Daring Diary of Captain Flashpowder*. The Creature would use its strength, ingenuity and friends within the creation community to gather the materials they needed (it ran both the Arts 'n' Crafts Club and the Creative Creations Collective Class). Then Arabella would direct the build by shouting very loudly at everyone.

"Faster, you lax 'n' lazy landlubbers! Pick up them feet or I'll make you walk the plank! And I'll make sure the waters are shark-infested!" she screamed, holding Pox by the tail as he gnashed and growled.

"YES, sir! I mean, MADAM! I mean…" replied the Creature, tramping past with a handful of wooden doors it had "borrowed" from various rooms around the castle.

"This is fun!" Arabella giggled.

A moment later, Stitch Head emerged with a large, carefully rolled piece of paper – his design for their ship.

"I finished!" he said. "What do you—"

"Speak up, bilge-brain!" yelled Arabella, snatching the design. "I don't want no mumbling unless I give you a direct mumbling order!" She unrolled the paper. "Why, I should have you swab the deck with your— Hey, that's really good!"

Arabella laid the design on the ground. It was a remarkably faithful copy of the *Gadabout*. Indeed, Stitch Head had named his ship the *Gadabout II*. A dark, imposing sail hung from the ship's mast and in its centre was the pirates' motif, the skull and crossbones, but with one notable difference – the skull was outlined with *stitches*.

"This is going to be a fine ship, Stitch Head," said Arabella with a smile. "I reckon you might have found your inner pirate, after all."

Stitch Head, Arabella and the Creature worked for a day and a night on the ship, stopping only for naps and food. The Creature was a particular fan of both, even though it didn't need either. Stitch Head, however, never stopped. He sawed, hammered, bolted and sewed as if his almost-life depended on it, all the while hoping that it would trigger something in his imagination — that it would reveal his inner pirate.

By the morning of the second day, the *Gadabout II* was complete. It was fair to say it didn't look exactly like Stitch Head's design. In fact, it didn't look *anything* like it.

"It's GREAT! The BESTEST pirate ship EVER!" hollered the Creature.

Stitch Head peered at the ship. It was a lot smaller than he'd hoped — only slightly bigger than the Creature — and its hull was cobbled together with random pieces of wood, clumsily nailed or tied. Even more noticeable were the sails — far from being vast, dark and imposing, they were a messy patchwork of floral-patterned bed sheets.

"Nah, it's a right old mess!" chuckled Arabella. "But it's a ship — *your* ship, Stitch Head. Why don't you try it out?"

Stitch Head climbed aboard, and the ship creaked and rattled as if it might fall to pieces at any moment. He edged cautiously to the bow, drew his sword and struck his most pirate-like pose. He tried to imagine the vast, blue oceans, the cool sea breeze, the distant islands...

"Onward … to adventure," he whispered, but to his disappointment, he felt no different. He was just a forgotten creation standing on a ramshackle boat. Stitch Head sighed. Perhaps it was for the best — if he could never leave the castle, why bother trying to pretend he was anything other than a forgotten creation?

"SO? Have you found your INNER pirate?" asked the Creature, clapping two of its three hands together in excitement. Stitch Head looked down at the expectant faces of his friends. He hated to lie, but they had worked so hard, he couldn't bear to tell them the truth. Finally, he said, "I-I think I have. I feel like Captain Flashpowder. Thank you … for everything. I guess I am part pirate, after all."

"I KNEW it!" boomed the Creature.

"Sounds like a job well done!" said Arabella. "Well, I'd best be heading back to Grubbers Nubbin. I ain't eaten nothing but sawdust and beetles all day – I'm *starving*..."

Arabella rubbed Pox on the belly and made him promise not to attack anyone until her next visit. He gave a reluctant "GRuKK!" and bit her on the ankle.

"Next time I come over, we're taking that thing down to Grubbers Harbour and setting sail," said Arabella, as she unlocked the Great Door. She heaved it open and made her way out.

"See you tomorro— Hang on, what's this?" She reappeared with something in her hand.

It was another letter.

THE SECOND LETTER

(Dear Stitch Head)

> *"Never trust a message in a bottle. Unless it's a treasure map."*
>
> From
> *The Daring Diary of Captain Flashpowder*

Stitch Head jumped down from the *Gadabout II* and took the letter. His jaw dropped as he stared at the front of the envelope.

To
Stitch Head
Castle Grotteskew
Grubbers Nubbin

"For ... me?" he whispered in horror. "But no one knows I even — I mean, no one knows about me. Except..."

"OPEN IT!" screamed the Creature. "Is it a LOVE letter? A GOLDEN ticket to a land of CHOCOLATE? The SUSPENSE is KILLING me!"

Stitch Head tore open the letter.

Dear Stitch Head
(and other monsters, creatures and mad things
of Castle Grotteskew),

I write to tell you that I have discovered a most
genuine life of fame, fortune and fulfillment in the
Outside World. In truth, everyone here considers me
a most esteemed fellow, and proclaims that my mad
professoring is the finest (and maddest) of all.
    I am famous!
    And so, I must tell you that I am abandoning my
life in the castle.
    I shall not return to Grotteskew, ever, ever again.
    Ever!
    Farewell, creations of Grotteskew! Long may
the castle loom above Grubbers Nubbin ... or crumble
to the ground. What do I care?
    I have forgotten you already!

Sincerely,
Mad Professor Erasmus

Stitch Head stared at the words, unable to breathe.

"What does it SAY? Have you won a PRIZE?" boomed the Creature. "I LOVE winning prizes! I expect—"

"Stitch Head, what is it?" asked Arabella, her voice suddenly soft. "What does it say?"

"He – he's gone," replied Stitch Head. "My master's not coming back."

Stitch Head slumped to his knees. He tried to read the letter again, but tears welled up in his eyes and blurred his vision. Under any other circumstances, he would have been delighted that the professor had chosen to write to him, of all the creations in the castle. But to abandon the castle … to abandon his work … to abandon *him*… Stitch Head felt anger and sadness bubbling up inside him.

"I don't UNDERSTAND," said the

Creature finally. "What does the OUTSIDE world have that the CASTLE doesn't? Apart from FRESH AIR, proper PLUMBING, and actual HUMAN beings…"

"Oh, forget the prof, Stitch Head – you don't need that crusty old castle-departer!" said Arabella, trying to cheer him up. "You've got your whole almost-life ahead of you! You don't want to spend it cleaning up after someone who hardly even knows you exist, right?"

"I-I…" whimpered Stitch Head, but in truth, that was exactly what he wanted. He wiped away his tears and got to his feet. "I'm sorry … I have to go."

"GO? Go WHERE?" asked the Creature.

"I-I don't know…" replied Stitch Head. He hurried out of the courtyard and disappeared into the enveloping gloom of the castle.

MOAT FLOAT

(Cheering up Stitch Head)

> *"When you're at the bottom of the ocean, the only way is up."*
>
> From
> *The Daring Diary of*
> *Captain Flashpowder*

Stitch Head wandered through the castle, feeling more lost and lonely than he had for years. He had no idea where he was going, or what he was going to do now he was a creation without a master. What's more, he felt as if he was seeing Grotteskew for the first time. The crumbling, stone walls, the bleak, unlit corridors, the vast, hollow chambers … it all seemed cold and unwelcoming.

He thought about returning to the dungeons of Grotteskew, far from the other creations, hoping that he might feel he belonged there. Or, at least, perhaps the darkness might swallow him…

But instead, he found himself in the Forgotten Room, sitting amongst the toys and books and dust. Perhaps the professor had been right to leave him there. Perhaps he never should have left. Perhaps this was where he belonged.

He didn't know how long he had been sitting there – minutes? hours? – when he heard a familiar sound...

"YaBBit!"

Stitch Head spun round to see Arabella standing in the doorway. Pox was perched on her shoulder, grumbling loudly.

"Thought I might find you here," said Arabella. "Ain't no good sitting around *moping*."

"Please," said Stitch Head, bowing his head. "I ... just leave me alone. I want to be alone."

"No chance," replied Arabella, sitting down next to him. "My nan always says the only thing worse than moping is getting your head kicked in by a horse – and she's done both in her time. You need cheering up, whether you like it or not."

"I really don't feel like—" began Stitch Head, but Arabella wasn't finished.

"The fact is, the professor's gone. Now you can sit here and wait for him to come back, just like you sat here all them years ... but he ain't coming back and you know it. You're free! And you're part pirate! There's a whole world out there — adventure and treasure and all sorts — all there for the taking!"

"I can't," replied Stitch Head. "I promised."

"Promised what? You can't protect him if he ain't here! I told you once and I'll tell you again — you gotta get out more."

"I can't!" repeated Stitch Head. "Last time I opened those gates the castle nearly fell! I trusted Fulbert Freakfinder because I wanted to be something I'm not... I'm a forgotten creation and that's all I'll ever—"

"No moping, I said!" snapped Arabella. She grabbed Stitch Head and pulled him towards the window. "I've got a surprise for you. See down there? In the moat?"

Stitch Head peered into the murk of the dusk. He could see the glistening waters of the castle moat that surrounded Grotteskew. And on the bank...

"Is ... is that the Creature?" whispered Stitch Head.

"It surely is! I gave it my key! First time beyond the castle walls, and loving it!" said Arabella, poking her head out of the window. "Oi, Creature!"

The Creature looked up at the window and gave a happy wave. Arabella gave it the thumbs up and it disappeared behind a large tree.

"Where's it going?" asked Stitch Head. After a moment, the Creature reappeared ... dragging the *Gadabout II* along the ground.

"Time you saw what you're missing," said Arabella. "We're going to show you the life you *could* have ... a life beyond these walls — a *pirate's* life."

Stitch Head watched in amazement as the Creature dragged the ship to the edge of the moat. Then, with an almighty shove, it pushed it into the water with a thunderous SPLOSH!

"A trusty ship!" said Arabella, as the *Gadabout II* bobbed about on the water. Despite its shape and put-together strangeness, it looked rather majestic. Perfect, perhaps, for a strange, put-together pirate.

It was then the water began to bubble, and the ship bobbed awkwardly. A moment later, it started to sink.

"OH, no no NO!" screamed the Creature. It jumped in after the ship, without realizing it couldn't swim. It flailed around for a moment before scrambling desperately back on to the bank, just in time to see the *Gadabout II* vanish beneath the water.

"*Huh*," grunted Arabella, as she watched the bow of the ship disappear into the moat. She turned to Stitch Head. "Any chance you didn't see that last bit?"

"Thank you for trying to cheer me up. I appreciate it, I really do," whispered Stitch Head. He looked around the Forgotten Room. "But I'm no pirate, eye or no eye. This is my almost-life, here, in the castle. *This* is all I've ever known. It's ... it's all I can imagine."

Arabella sighed. "I have to go home," she said. "But I'll be back soon, all right? And if you need anything, you know where I'll be."

"Thank you," Stitch Head replied. He watched Arabella leave, and then sat back down amongst the toys and the books and the dust.

THE PIRATE'S EYE

(The Creature gives Stitch Head a present)

> *"You've never seen the world until you've seen it through an eyepatch."*
>
> From
> *The Daring Diary of*
> *Captain Flashpowder*

Stitch Head had been sitting in the Forgotten Room for a few hours, watching the sun set through the window. At the very moment dusk was about to fall, a crumpled envelope dropped from above and landed next to him. He felt his heart skip. *Another* letter? Could it be from the professor? He looked up and saw a conspicuous shape peering over the hole in the ceiling. The shape disappeared into the shadows with a giggle, and Stitch Head realized immediately that it was the Creature. What was it up to? Was it some sort of game? He picked up the envelope and opened it, finding a note inside.

DEAR STICH HEAD
SORRY ABOWT SINKING YOUR
PIRATE SHIP!
ARABELA SAID YOU WONTED
TO BE ALONE.

BUT I THORT YOU MIGHT
LIKE A PRESENT.
(IT'S SOMETHING YOU DIDN'T
PUT ON YOR LIST.)
I HOPE IT HELLPS!
YOR BESTEST FREND,
THE CREATURE

Stitch Head looked inside the envelope. There was a long strip of black cloth, thin at each end but wider in the middle. He took it out and inspected it. At first he had no idea what it could be, but then it struck him...

It was an *eyepatch*.

Stitch Head shook his head. It was too late for eyepatches and pirates and adventures.

Nevertheless, he was grateful that the Creature had tried to help – and felt rather guilty that it had gone to all that effort. He smiled faintly, and then found himself covering his left eye with the eyepatch and tying it round his head. For the first time, he saw the world only out of his ice-blue eye.

Slowly, the gloom of the castle seemed to lift. The fading light of dusk was replaced with a bright, white light that seemed to burst through every crack and crevice. The dark, stone walls appeared to melt away, and in their place stretched the endless, glimmering ocean. Stitch Head looked up to see the ceiling vanish to reveal the bright, morning sky. It was as if the Forgotten Room had disappeared. In his mind's eye, Stitch Head saw the white crests of the crashing waves, the spiralling light of the midday sun, the gulls soaring above him and singing his name. He felt the warm ocean spray on his face as his grand pirate ship rose and crashed through the water, sailing proudly towards an island filled with untold riches – and adventure.

"I can see it! I can see it *all*," whispered Stitch Head. In that moment, he felt freer than he ever had … and he *knew* he was a pirate.

Stitch Head raced through the castle, his patch over his eye and his sword by his side.

"Creature! Creature! I can see it now! I'm part pirate!" he cried, as he hurried down corridor after corridor. He found the Creature in a large chamber in the south wing playing a card game with a tin-plated turkey and a wheel-footed wolf-woman.

"The eyepatch – it worked!" cried Stitch Head. "All I had to do was look at things through Flashpowder's eye!"

"GREAT!" said the Creature, not entirely sure what that meant. "I'm SO glad we can FINALLY play PIRATES now!"

"What's the point of playing? What's the point of me staying here at all if the professor has gone for ever? And if he's not here to make any more creations, I don't have to worry about making any more cures!" replied Stitch Head. He suddenly noticed the other creations in the room. For the first time in his almost-life, he didn't feel the slightest need to stay hidden.

"Sorry to interrupt," he said with a smile.

"Interrupt away, my young fellow," replied the wolf-woman. "I have the most awful hand of cards, anyway."

"Creature, I'm ready!" continued Stitch Head. "I'm ready to sail the several seas! I'm ready for adventure! We need to get my ship!"

"Umm… I THINK I might have DEFINITELY sunk it," said the Creature.

"Don't worry," replied Stitch Head. "I've got an idea."

RAISING THE GADABOUT II

(Just whistle)

> *"You can never have too much gold! Unless it makes your ship sink."*
>
> From
> *The Daring Diary of*
> *Captain Flashpowder*

For the second time in his almost-life, Stitch Head opened the Great Door and stepped out into the night air. But this time, there was no Fulbert Freakfinder waiting for him on the other side. Stitch Head saw a world of possibility and adventure. That was the world through a pirate's eye — the world that Captain Flashpowder must have seen.

Stitch Head adjusted his eyepatch, and then he and the Creature hurried down to the bank of the moat.

"Time to call in a favour," said Stitch Head. He put two fingers in his mouth and whistled.

"*Fw-p-p-pp!*"

It wasn't so much of a whistle as a strange, wet rasp — like a cat farting.

"That could be a problem," muttered Stitch Head. "I've never tried to whistle before."

"Wait, are you WHISTLING? I LOVE whistling!" boomed the Creature. "The OTHER creations won't let me DO it because it makes their TEETH fall out ... the ones that HAVE teeth."

The Creature put two fingers in its mouth — from each of its three hands — and blew!

"ThWwWEEEEEooooooEEEP!"

The sound made Stitch Head's stitches ache. He covered his ears as the whistle rang out through the air.

"That should do it…" he whimpered, and peered into the moat. After a moment, the water began to bubble and churn. Then, slowly, something started to emerge.

"The *Gadabout II*!" cried the Creature, as Stitch Head's ship slowly rose from the depths. "Am I DOING this? Do I have a MAGIC whistle?"

"I don't think so…" whispered Stitch Head. By now, the *Gadabout II* was back on the surface of the water, leaking from numerous gaps in the hull. But it didn't stop rising until it was clear of the water entirely. Wrapped around the base of the hull, were eight long tentacles.

"It's him…" whispered Stitch Head, a smile spreading across his face.

"Him? Him WHO?"

"Him! I mean it! I mean the octo-monster!"

"A good evening to you, my fellow creations!" said the octo-monster, as it hoisted the *Gadabout II* out of the water and on to the bank. "I assume you've come to collect your rather fetching vessel…"

"Thanks, uh…" began Stitch Head.

"Call me Updike — at your most obedient service," replied the octo-monster. "And it's the very least I can do to thank you for bringing me to my senses. Enjoy your ship! Although ... I feel duty bound to point out there are one or two rather large holes in the hull. Did you not intend it to float?"

"It's ... a work-in-progress," replied Stitch Head, plugging a hole in the ship's hull with his finger. "But it *will* float, I promise. Thanks, Updike."

Stitch Head and the Creature spent the next few hours getting the *Gadabout II* ship-shape and leak-proof. After another, more successful float-test in the moat, Stitch Head was ready to set sail.

Almost.

"It's so *far*," whispered Stitch Head, staring out across the moonlit landscape. "The ocean seemed much closer from up in the castle. I've barely been outside the Great Door and now look at me! Trying to move a ship to the ocean!"

"Don't WORRY, I've got it COVERED," said the Creature. It grabbed the *Gadabout II* in its two mightiest arms, and with one powerful heave, hoisted the ship on to its back.

"GNNNFFF!" grunted the Creature. "Right! To the OCEAN! Via ADVENTURE! And Grubbers Nubbin."

"Creature ... you'd do that for me? Leave Grotteskew? Carry the ship all the way to the sea?"

"Well, you're NOT going to be much of a PIRATE without a CRUSTY CREW, now, ARE you?" replied the Creature.

"A crusty – trusty crew?" said Stitch Head. "You mean—"

"I MEAN I want to be a PIRATE, too!

I'm SICK of tea parties! I want to go on a GREAT ADVENTURE with my BESTEST friend. What do you SAY?"

"I say … great!" said Stitch Head.

"Great? GREAT! We were HOPING you'd agree…" boomed the Creature gleefully. It put two fingers (from its unoccupied third arm) into its mouth and—

"ThWEEEoooEEP!"

A moment later, Pox swooped down from a perch on the castle's parapets, yapping and growling. He landed on the ground next to Stitch Head and hissed angrily in his face.

"Uh, Creature?" Stitch Head whispered. "I don't think I need a trusty companion…"

"It's not FOR you," replied the Creature. "Arabella said she'd ONLY come with us if we BROUGHT him along."

A TRUSTY CREW

(Let's get this show on the sea)

> "There's no crew like
> a trusty crew."
>
> From
> *The Daring Diary of
> Captain Flashpowder*

Under the cover of darkness, Stitch Head, the Creature (carrying the *Gadabout II* upon its back) and their "trusty" companion, Pox, made the slow trek to Grubbers Nubbin to collect the last member of the crew.

Stitch Head had always been nervous of the land beyond the castle. It was so open — it felt as if there was nowhere to hide. But tonight, through his pirate's eye, the world without walls looked like an adventure waiting to happen.

They crept towards the outskirts of

Grubbers Nubbin, a few faint lamplights still burning in the sleeping town.

"I hope no one SPOTS us," said the Creature. "I don't want to give anyone a FRIGHT. Last time I saw my reflection in the bath water I SCREAMED for an HOUR."

"Ha! I've had scarier knee scabs," said Arabella, stepping out from behind a tree.

"SwaRRTiKi!" yapped Pox happily. He flew towards Arabella and landed on her head. Then he immediately started chewing her hair.

"Arabella! How did you know we were coming?" asked Stitch Head.

Arabella shook her head. "The Creature, carrying a ship on its back? I saw that coming a *mile* away. I've been watching out for you... I knew you'd come round eventually. Right, let's get this show on the road! I mean, sea."

"Arabella, are — are you sure about this?" asked Stitch Head. "I don't know how long we'll be gone. Your life here ... your nan..."

"My nan? She don't even know what *day* it is. She don't know who I am half the time," said Arabella with a shrug. "Anyway, I haven't had a proper adventure in months, so if you're planning on setting sail, you'd better make room for me and my brand-new *pirating* boots."

Stitch Head smiled broadly.

"Welcome aboard."

GRUBBERS HARBOUR

(The voice on the wind)

> *"Sail away, sail away, sail away!"*
>
> From
> *The Daring Diary of
> Captain Flashpowder*

With his trusty crew complete, Stitch Head felt more ready than ever for a pirate's life. They crept through the cobbled streets of Grubbers Nubbin and followed the winding road down to the sea. Dawn was beginning to break over the horizon when Stitch Head smelled the sharp, salty air of the ocean.

They had arrived at Grubbers Harbour.

The sea was even more magnificent than it had been in Stitch Head's imagination. It stretched endlessly into the distance – a great, gleaming ocean of possibility. Who knew what adventures were waiting for him out there?

"Right, let's get this party started!" said Arabella.

In the near distance was a rounded bay, filled with a dozen or more boats and ships. At the far end of the harbour, several hefty sailors were loading a large ship with cargo.

Stitch Head and his trusty crew were careful not to be seen as they hurried down to the bay and along a wooden walkway that jutted out into the sea. As soon as they reached the end, the Creature hefted the *Gadabout II* off its shoulders and deposited it in the water.

"It STILL floats!" it cried happily. For a moment, they all watched the ship bob about.

"Well, don't just stand there gawping, landlubbers!" said Arabella.

She jumped into the ship, followed by the Creature, who took up almost the whole deck. For a moment, Stitch Head paused. Then...

"Hoist the middle mast!" he cried, leaping aboard. He grabbed the ship's wheel and did his best to steer as the tide carried them out to sea.

"We did it," cried Stitch Head, looking back. In the far distance he could just make out the distant spires of Castle Grotteskew. "Onward … to *adventure*."

He cast his pirate's eye out to sea, and felt the chill air whistle past his ears. It sounded like a voice, as if the ocean itself was whispering to him.

"Unhand me, you fiends!"

Oddly, the ocean sounded rather like his master.

"I said, unhand me! I'm too important to be manhandled!"

"Master…?" he whispered. He could have *sworn* he heard the professor.

"You OK, Stitch Head?" asked the Creature, trying to find a place to sit on the tiny ship.

Stitch Head looked back and peered across

the bay to the large ship. On the ship's ramp, two men were arguing. He could only see one of them clearly – he was a tall, broad-shouldered man with a thick, black beard. The other was short and fat with spindly legs. He was dragging a large sack that writhed and squirmed.

As the *Gadabout II* bobbed out of the bay, Stitch Head strained to hear what the men were saying.

"Now, see here, it took me an *age* to book a ship that would take *any* cargo! No questions asked, you said!"

"A human being is not cargo! I be the cap'n of this ship, by criminy! It be my neck on the line if we're caught..."

"It's more money you're after, is it? Lugs and mumbles, you drive a hard bargain, cap'n!"

Stitch Head watched as the fat man handed "the cap'n" a wad of money. The cap'n nodded, and the fat man began hefting the sack on to the edge of one of the empty crates. As he turned, Stitch Head finally got a look at his face. His eye grew wide. Including the professor, Stitch Head had only met three people in his almost-life ... *and the fat man was one of them.*

"*Fulbert Freakfinder...!*" he whispered, his mouth agape.

Stitch Head watched as Freakfinder emptied out the sack. A bony, silver-haired old man fell out and tumbled into the crate.

"Ooooof! You can't treat me like this! I'm an award-winning mad professor!"

It was Professor Erasmus.

FOLLOW THAT SHIP

(Stitch Head sets sail)

*"The journey to adventure
is paved with ocean."*

From
*The Daring Diary of
Captain Flashpowder*

Stitch Head stared in horror as Fulbert Freakfinder locked the professor inside the crate.

"Sh-ship ... Master ... Freakfinder!" Stitch Head stuttered.

"Are you OK, Stitch Head?" asked the Creature, rocking the *Gadabout II* as it struggled to get comfy.

"Yeah, what are you on about? You ain't making no sense," said Arabella.

"Fulbert Freakfinder has kidnapped the professor, and he's on that ship!" cried Stitch Head, snapping out of his daze. They watched the ship raise anchor and begin to pull out of the harbour. Stitch Head grabbed the wheel and turned it frantically. "We have to save him! Hoist the sail, quick!"

"FILBERT FREAKFINDER? Are you SURE?" asked the Creature. "As in THE

Filbert Freakfinder, your ARCH-enemy?"

"Yes, it's *Fulbert* Freakfinder, I'm sure!" yelled Stitch Head, steering the *Gadabout II* towards the horizon. "Follow that ship!"

"I thought I gave the orders around here…" said Arabella, releasing the mainsail's bindings. The ragged, patchwork sail unfurled and caught a strong current of air. With a WHOMPH! the *Gadabout II* lurched and nodded as they were buffeted out to sea.

"Hang on to something! The wind's on our backs!" cried Arabella. The *Gadabout II* sped across the waves, rattling and creaking as if it was about to come apart. Stitch Head hung on for dear almost-life, his pirate's eye fixed on the other ship.

"What's FREAKFINDER doing on a SHIP with the PROFESSOR?" shouted the Creature through the wind.

"I don't know . . . but I know what he *wants* with him," said Stitch Head grimly. "Freakfinder needs mad things for his *Travelling Carnival of Unnatural Wonders*. He's going to force the professor to create made-to-order freaks."

"That pig-faced plotter!" snapped Arabella. "How did he get his hairy hands on the prof?"

"The award! Freakfinder must have been watching the castle . . . or he knew the professor was leaving – but how? Memories flashed through Stitch Head's mind like lightning. He took the two letters out of his sleeve and unfolded them. His eye darted to the bottom of the first letter. . .

Professor K. E. Farfriend, DMP (Doctor of Mad Professoring) . . .

"K. E. Farfriend. . ." he muttered. Slowly, the letters began to un-jumble. . .

F
K
E
A
N
F
R   I

E   R

D

"FREAKFINDER!" bellowed the Creature. Stitch Head and Arabella stared in disbelief. "I play a LOT of SCRABBLE," the Creature added proudly.

"No, *no*... I've been such an idiot," said Stitch Head, holding both letters next to each other. "I couldn't see what was right in front of my eye ... these letters are from *Fulbert Freakfinder.*"

"SwARtiKi?" yapped Pox.

"Yeah, what *are* you on about?" asked Arabella.

"It's a trick ... it's all been a trick!" cried Stitch Head. He held up the letters. "Freakfinder wrote the first letter to lure the professor out of the castle so he could kidnap him! Then he sent the *second* letter from the professor – to stop us from going after him. They're even in the same handwriting – look!"

"So THAT means…" began the Creature.

"It means we have to save him!" cried Stitch Head.

"That big ol' ship is getting away twice as fast as we're gaining on it," said Arabella. "We ain't *never* going to catch it at this rate."

Sure enough, the other ship, with its dozen impressive-looking sails, was speeding away across the water.

"We have to go faster!" cried Stitch Head.

"We can't!" said Arabella. "This is as fast as we go unless we drop some weight!"

"We don't have anything to drop!" replied Stitch Head. "There's no room for anything on this ship but us! Master…" For a moment he thought he could hear the professor's cries … but it was just the sound of the wind.

"Less WEIGHT, huh?" said the Creature finally. It put one of its three hands on Stitch Head's shoulder. "Rescue your master. I KNOW you can do it. I BELIEVE in you. Remember … you're a PIRATE now."

The Creature got to its feet, pinched its nose with its third hand … and threw itself overboard.

SPLOOOOooooSH!

"Creature! No!" cried Stitch Head.

"What are BESTEST friends for?" cried the Creature, gurgling as it tried to stay afloat.

"We can't leave you! You can't even *swim!*" said Stitch Head.

"All the more REASON to practise my DOGGY-paddle," replied the Creature, frantically thrashing all three of its arms. "Now GO!"

Stitch Head had little choice. Without the Creature, the *Gadabout II* was half as heavy – a decent gust of wind was all it took to send it speeding across the water. Within moments, they were gaining on the other ship ... and the Creature was a speck in the ocean.

ALL ABOARD

(High jinks on the high seas)

*"I've never met a ship
I didn't want to board."*

From
*The Daring Diary of
Captain Flashpowder*

Stitch Head held on like never before as the *Gadabout II* sped through the waves.

"Creature…" said Stitch Head. "Do – do you think it's going to be OK?"

"No good crying about it now – we're gaining on the ship!" said Arabella. "Get your head back in the game! You're a *pirate* now."

"I'm a pirate now…" Stitch Head repeated, and turned back to the horizon.

He steered the ship and felt the wind on the back of his head driving them on. The *Gadabout II* bounced and careered along the surface of the water like a stone. With the extra speed, they were quickly catching up with the other ship – and the professor. Before long, they drew level.

"It's now or never," cried Stitch Head. "Arabella, grab the wheel! Bring us in as close as you can!"

Arabella grabbed the ship's wheel and turned it to the left. The *Gadabout II* bobbed closer to the hull of the other ship, closer and closer, until Stitch Head feared the two ships might crash together.

"Now what?" said Arabella, trying to hold the ship steady.

"What would Captain Flashpowder do?" murmered Stitch Head to himself. He cast his pirate's eye down to the broken sword tucked into his belt. An idea came to him, like a flash of light. He quickly untied the sail rope and rolled it up. Then he drew his sword and tied it to one end of the rope.

"GLukK!" barked Pox.

"Whatever you're going to do, do it now!" cried Arabella.

Stitch Head started swinging the rope round his head – faster and faster, until it filled the air with a shrill whistling sound – and then flung it as hard as he could! The broken sword flew through the air, clunking on to the deck of the other ship. Stitch Head yanked the rope and felt the sword catch and hold fast on the deck.

"As soon as you let go of the wheel, grab on to me!" cried Stitch Head, gripping the rope tightly. He peered over the edge into the churning water and adjusted his eyepatch. "We have to swing for it! Prepare for boarding!"

"*Now* you're talking," said Arabella. She let go of the ship's wheel and grabbed hold of Stitch Head's tiny shoulders as the *Gadabout II* began to veer away. Stitch Head closed his eye – and leaped from the ship! They swung across the water, crashing hard into the hull of the other ship. Stitch Head clung on for dear almost-life, his stitches fit to burst as Arabella locked her elbows round his neck. He quickly realized he hadn't the strength to carry them up the rope…

"YaBBiT!" growled Pox, as he flitted around them. Stitch Head opened his eye to see Arabella grasp the rope above his head and clamber over him. She shimmied to the top and scrambled over the side of the ship on to the deck. Then she leaned back over and held out her hand.

"We ain't got all day – grab on!" she whispered. Stitch Head reached up and clasped Arabella's hand. She pulled with all her might, hauling him on to the deck.

"Thanks...!" whispered Stitch Head, untying his sword from the rope.

"Nice swinging – you're really getting the hang of this pirate stuff," she replied, as Pox landed on her shoulder.

The ship was *huge*. Stitch Head ushered Arabella behind a large barrel on the side of the deck. He peered out from behind it and looked around. They were halfway between the bow, at the front of the ship, and the stern. The rear of the wooden deck was piled high with crates, caskets and barrels, while the bow crawled with a dozen burly-looking crewmen. Above them, a spider's web of rigging stretched high amongst the billowing sails.

"So, what now?" Arabella asked.

Stitch Head's ice-blue eye glinted in the brightening sunlight.

"Now we find the professor."

CRATE EXPECTATIONS

(Finding the professor)

> *"A true pirate always
> keeps his buckles swashed."*
>
> From
> *The Daring Diary of
> Captain Flashpowder*

"Pox, fly up to the rigging and stay out of sight," said Stitch Head, as they huddled behind the barrel. "Wait there and watch for my signal."

Pox stared at Stitch Head and then snarled angrily at him.

"Uh, please?" he asked nervously.

"Do what he says, you grump, or no hair chewing for a week," said Arabella. Pox grunted sulkily and flew up into the sails.

"Right, I say we go in, all boots kicking," said Arabella, tightening her laces. "I'm in the mood to—"

"Let me out this very moment! I'll miss the award ceremony!"

"It's the professor!" whispered Stitch Head. "Arabella — he's in one of those crates! Follow me ... and *please* don't pick a fight with anyone quite yet."

Arabella gave a huffy nod and followed Stitch Head. They crept silently along the edge of the deck towards the crates, ducking between barrels and lifeboats. Stitch Head craned his head to listen over the sound of the whistling wind.

"Release me, I command you! I'm getting cramp in my professoring hand!"

"This way ... no, *that* way," said Stitch Head, moving along the huge stack of crates. He clambered up on to one, then another.

"You'll regret this! I'm well known for my madness!"

"Doesn't he ever shut up?" said Arabella, as she kept a lookout from the deck.

At the top of the pile sat a crate that rattled and shook. "Un-crate me this moment! I must return to my laboratory!"

"Professor, it's all right, we're here!" said Stitch Head, reaching the crate. It's Stitch Head! We're here to rescue you!"

The crate stopped rattling.

"Who?" asked the professor.

"Stitch Head ... your *first creation*. We've travelled the several seas to find you..."

"Stitch Head ... Stitch Head ... sort of rings a bell..." mumbled the professor.

Stitch Head sighed. He suddenly felt smaller than ever for imagining that his master would remember him ... but then *he* remembered something.

Only *he* had the pirate's eye.

"Sit tight, master, we're going to get you out of there!" said Stitch Head boldly. "We're going to get you back to Castle Grotteskew, where—"

"Lugs and mumbles, it can't be … *Stitch Head*?" Stitch Head spun round and looked down at the deck. The fat face of Fulbert Freakfinder was staring back at him.

FIENDISH FULBERT FREAKFINDER

(What would Captain Flashpowder do?)

> *"If in doubt, draw your sword!"*
>
> From
> *The Daring Diary of Captain Flashpowder*

"We've been rumbled! Let's get kicking!" cried Arabella.

"Impossible…" gasped Fulbert Freakfinder. He pointed his cane at Stitch Head. "How did you work out my most excellent plan? It was foolproof! Why, all that effort I went to *forging* that letter from Professor Erasmus…"

Stitch Head suddenly felt a burning need to confess the truth – that he had simply stumbled across Freakfinder's fiendish plot … that he had chosen the life of a pirate over his master – but Arabella was quick to speak her mind.

"Yeah, well, your rotten plan was a load of stinky rubbish, cos here we are!" she shouted. "You didn't even bother to change your handwriting, stupid fatty pig-face!"

"I remember you, too, you rude little snot," hissed Freakfinder. "But I must admit, I'm impressed … leavin' the castle, trackin' me

down, smugglin' yourselves aboard the ship…
But what's your plan now, Stitch Head? Save
your precious master and swim back to shore?
Ha! Lugs and mumbles, you're fools!"

"You scheming slug! I'll kick that smug
grin off your face!" growled Arabella.

"I believe you might try, little snot … but
then, you can't kick us *all*," said Freakfinder.
He took a deep breath and yelled, "Intruders!
Stowaways! Sound the alarm!"

"Oh *no* … Arabella! Up here! Climb!"
cried Stitch Head.

Arabella huffed and clambered up the
crates, as a dozen crewmen appeared from
below decks, each burlier than the last. They
gathered round the stack of crates, grinding
teeth and cracking knuckles. On the other side
of the crates was the edge of the ship, and a
long fall to a watery grave.

"Stowaways, be it? And *children*, at that."
The tall, bearded man from the harbour
stepped through the crowd and peered up at
them. "Well, I be *cap'n* of this vessel, so what
I say goes. Down you get off there. I'm sure
your parents are worried sick about you." He
peered at Stitch Head. "Especially you – you
look like you should be in hospital!"

"Leave them to me, cap'n," sneered
Freakfinder. "I shall ensure that they never
bother you again."

"Try it, you podgy pig!" snapped Arabella.

"Wait, do you know these characters,
Freakfinder?" asked the cap'n.

"That I do, cap'n. That patchwork rag doll
calls himself Stitch Head, would you believe."
Freakfinder gave a little chuckle. "The eyepatch
is new, though. You playin' at pirates now,
Stitch Head?"

"I … I'm not playing," replied Stitch Head.

"These little snots think they have some claim over my precious cargo," said Freakfinder, pointing to the crate with his cane. "They're *thieves*, come to steal from your ship, cap'n."

"Take that back, hog-neck!" yelled Arabella.

"Thieves, eh?" said the cap'n suspiciously. "We'll see. Potts! Chump! Bring them down here and lock them in the hold."

As the crewmen advanced, even Arabella looked nervous.

"What would Captain Flashpowder do?" Stitch Head whispered to himself. His ice-blue eye gleamed like never before. He drew his broken sword and held it aloft.

"My name is Stitch Head, and I *am* a pirate!" he cried. "I have travelled the ocean wide to take back what is mine! My quarrel is with Fulbert Freakfinder. Return his cargo to me, or face the consequences!"

For a long moment, there was stunned silence aboard the ship. Then laughter rang out across the deck.

"Lugs and mumbles, who did you borrow your backbone from?" Freakfinder laughed. "Well, don't just stand there – get 'em!"

"You asked for it," said Stitch Head. "Pox! Now!"

Stitch Head looked up into the sails to see Pox perched on the rigging, defiantly still. Stitch Head turned to Arabella. "Uh, would you mind...?"

"No bother," said Arabella with a grin. "Pox! It's feeding time!"

STITCH HEAD VS FREAKFINDER

(Feeding time)

> *"An adventure a day keeps
> the doctor away!
> Unless you get stabbed."*
>
> From
> *The Daring Diary of
> Captain Flashpowder*

"GRAA–ARHH!"

As fast as lightning, Pox swooped down into the crowd of crewmen. He growled madly, biting arms and legs, tearing out hair and shredding clothes. The panicked crew scattered as the crazed creation attacked them with all his monstrous fury.

"My eyes!"

"My hair!"

"My trousers!"

"Yes! It's *kick o'clock*!" cried Arabella. She leaped down from the crates and started booting anything that moved.

Stitch Head turned his attention to the crate. He jammed his sword into the lock and tried to prise it open.

"I'll ... save you ... master...!"

"Oh no, you don't!" growled Freakfinder, clambering up the crates. "Try to take what's mine, will you?"

Stitch Head turned round in time to see Freakfinder swing his cane. He ducked and the cane came crashing down on the professor's crate.

"Thieving snot! I'll knock your head off!" yelled Freakfinder, banging the crate with his cane. Stitch Head dodged left, then right, desperately avoiding the blows — and found himself balanced precariously on the edge of the stack. He glanced behind him at the long drop into the sea.

"Nowhere left to run! That'll teach you to play at pirates," sneered Freakfinder. He swung his cane back and forth, closing in on Stitch Head. Stitch Head threw himself at Freakfinder and skidded between his legs. He grabbed his wooden sword out of the crate's lock and rounded on Freakfinder.

"HA! What's that supposed to be?" Freakfinder cackled.

"That," replied Stitch Head firmly, "is my trusty sword. And I'm not playing. I *am* a pirate."

Stitch Head launched himself at Freakfinder. Sword clashed against cane! Stitch Head felt his tiny bones rattle under the impact. Freakfinder was so much bigger and stronger than he was. He parried two more blows, but could barely keep hold of his sword – his stitches were strained to breaking point.

"Hold still!" howled Freakfinder. "Hold still while I bash you!"

But Stitch Head kept moving, weaving in and out of Freakfinder's legs. Before long, Freakfinder began puffing and panting.

"Snot … hold … still!" he gasped breathlessly. This was Stitch Head's chance! He jumped over Freakfinder's cane and on to the professor's crate. Then raised his sword…

"Who's out there? Release me, I say!" protested the professor, rattling the crate with all his might. As Stitch Head struggled to keep his footing, Freakfinder lunged with the last of his strength. He struck hard with his cane, knocking Stitch Head's sword out of his hand. It spun and whirled high into the air.

"Not so … swashbucklin' … now!" puffed Freakfinder. Stitch Head's eye darted upwards to his spinning sword. Suddenly, he sprang towards Freakfinder! He grabbed him by the ears and scrambled up his hat until he reached the top. As Freakfinder flailed and cursed, stumbling fowards, Stitch Head somersaulted into the air!

As he spun and spiralled, time itself seemed to slow down. Stitch Head saw the polished wood of the deck, and then the billowing clouds and the white light of the sun. Then, as he landed back on the crate, he raised his hand — and his still-spinning sword fell into his palm.

"*Told* you it was trusty," whispered Stitch Head. He swung his sword, knocking Freakfinder's cane over the side of the ship and into the sea.

"Lugs … and … mumbles!" panted Freakfinder. He gripped his chest and fell to his knees. "You'll give me a … heart attack … with all this … horseplay!"

Stitch Head's eye glinted in the sunlight. He placed his sword under Freakfinder's chin.

"Open that crate and free my master," he said. "Do it, now, or I swear I'll—"

"Get off me! I'll kick your knees off!"

"Arabella?" said Stitch Head. He wheeled round to see the cap'n holding her in mid-air by the scruff of the neck. The other crewmen, scarred and chewed from their battle with Pox, had managed to throw a sack over the mad monkey-bat.

"Leave her alone!" he cried. "I mean it!"

"I give the orders round here, by criminy!" hollered the cap'n. "Now drop your sword and come down from there!"

"Don't do it, Stitch Head!" screamed Arabella, kicking out wildly.

"Hush, you! You near broke my shin with all that kicking," growled the cap'n, slapping her across the face with his free hand.

"No! Please don't hurt her!" cried Stitch Head, throwing his trusty sword to the deck.

"That's better! Now let's be rid of them!" howled Freakfinder. He grabbed Stitch Head, hoisting him into the air and dangling him over the side of the ship.

"Hang on a minute, Freakfinder," said the cap'n. "No one said anything about drowning children! I may be unscrupulous, but I have my scruples…"

"He's no child … he's a monster! A freak! Escaped from a lunatic asylum — just like the old man in the crate!"

"That's a lie!" cried Stitch Head. "Please — we've not escaped from *anywhere*. Freakfinder *kidnapped* the professor — who *is* mad, but in a mad professoring sort of way — and he means to use him to make horrors for his freak show!"

"Lugs and mumbles, you've got a big mouth for a little snot," snarled Freakfinder. "I ain't about to have you ruin my chance at fame and fortune…"

"Freakfinder — don't!" cried the cap'n — but it was too late. Freakfinder hurled Stitch Head into the sea.

CREATION OVERBOARD

(Let's play "pirates")

"Overboard is underrated."

From
*The Daring Diary of
Captain Flashpowder*

"WaAHHH!" screamed Stitch Head, as he plummeted towards the ocean. His strange, lonely, almost-life flashed before his eye – and he wondered if even Captain Flashpowder would know what to do. But, just as he expected to crash into the water...

KRUMP!

"Oww!" cried Stitch Head. He'd never fallen into the sea before, but this didn't feel like water *at all*.

"Welcome ABOARD!" came a cry. Stitch Head stared up into the grinning face of the Creature. He glanced about in disbelief. He was on the *Gadabout II*!

"Creature!" cried Stitch Head. "What? How? You're all right!"

"BETTER than all right!" it boomed, wringing out its sodden coat. "I discovered I'm the BESTEST SWIMMER ever! I'm like a

MERMAID! Or Mer-CREATURE ... did you know I had GILLS? They're GREAT! So there I was, practising my DOGGY-PADDLE, when I came across the *GADABOUT II* in the water... And since you weren't in it..."

"Creature, you're *amazing!*" cried Stitch Head.

"All in a day's PIRATING, Captain Stitch Head!" it said, saluting Stitch Head. Stitch Head saluted back, and then pointed up at the big ship.

"Speaking of pirates," said Stitch Head, "we still need to rescue the rest of our trusty crew…"

"GREAT!" cried the Creature, scooping Stitch Head up in its third hand and leaping from the *Gadabout II*! It dug its free hands into the thick wood of the ship's hull and began scaling the side. It reached the top in moments and flung itself on to the deck.

"AARR! LANDLUBBLERS BEWARE! I'M IN A PIRATING MOOD!" it roared, waving its three arms and tail.

The crewmen froze.

"M-m-m-MONSTER!" screamed one.

"Actually, it's CREATURE," it replied. "Until I think of something BETTER, that is… ARR!"

The crewmen's shrill screams filled the air as they scattered in terror!

"HEY, everyone's REALLY getting into CHARACTER," noted the Creature as it placed Stitch Head on the deck. "GREAT! I'd better PULL something really PIRATEY out of my hat…"

The Creature roared its most impressively *piratey* "AARRRR!" yet and began chasing the crewmen around the ship, crying "I'll SHIVER your TIMBERS!"

"Go get 'em," cried Stitch Head, grabbing his sword from the deck.

"Criminy, this be madness!" wailed the cap'n, dropping Arabella. She immediately kicked him hard in the shin and he crumpled to the ground.

"Stitch Head! You ain't looking half as drowned as I thought you would," said Arabella, watching the Creature pursue the terrified crewmen around the deck.

Stitch Head's eye darted upwards to the stack of crates – and his master. The crate was still there, but...

"Where's Freakfinder?" Stitch Head whispered.

"Lugs and mumbles, don't let it get me!" came the terrified cry. Stitch Head looked up and up ... until he spotted Freakfinder climbing the rigging. He clambered all the way up and wrapped his spindly arms round the nearest mast.

"Allow me," said Arabella. She pulled open the sack containing the growling, thrashing Pox and emptied him out. He shook with mad rage and looked for something to attack. Arabella pointed up at the mast and grinned.

"Get that fat pig, there's a good monkey-bat!"

RESCUING THE PROFESSOR

(The cap'n's favourite book)

> *"Invest in adventure!"*
>
> From
> *The Daring Diary of*
> *Captain Flashpowder*

It wasn't long before Stitch Head and his trusty crew had taken over the ship. Pox quickly dislodged Fulbert Freakfinder from the mast (sending him crashing to the deck with an almighty KRU-DUMP!) and the Creature dumped him with the cap'n and crew, who huddled on the deck in fear.

"That was GREAT!" boomed the Creature, looming over the sailors as Pox flitted around them, snapping his jaws. "PIRATES is SO much better than TEA PARTIES! AARRRR!"

Stitch Head and Arabella clambered back up on to the crates. They prised open the top-most one and the professor popped out like a jack-in-the-box, frantic and flailing.

"Foul villainy! Beastly fiends! I am kidnapped! You cannot keep me from my laboratory! I have creations simmering!"

"Master, it's all right, you're safe now," said Stitch Head. "It's me! It's – it's Stitch Head."

"Who?" asked the professor again.

"Oh, f'goodness' sake! Back in your box, you ungrateful old lizard!" said Arabella and slammed the lid on the professor.

"Arabella! What are you doing?" cried Stitch Head.

"I reckon if a mad professor don't even

recognize his first creation, he don't deserve no fresh air," she said. "He'll be all right in there for a while. Anyway, do you want to tell the prof that he ain't got no award waiting for him?"

"Uh, I suppose not," replied Stitch Head. He gave a faint smile and breathed a long, slow sigh of relief. His master was safe – and that was enough for now.

"So WHAT should we DO with THEM?" asked the Creature, striking its most pirate-like pose in front of the terrified crew. "Oooo! Let's make them WALK the PLANK! NOTHING'S more PIRATEY than PLANK-walking…"

"Please don't do us harm!" cried the cap'n. "We are but humble sailors, trying to make an honest living!"

"Ain't nothing honest about kidnapping a crusty old geezer," said Arabella.

"We were led astray! Freakfinder ain't no friend of ours!" cried the cap'n.

"Lugs and mumbles, I want my money back, you – you backstabbing pirates!" grumbled Freakfinder.

"We can't listen to this all day – we've got a world of adventure ahead of us," said Arabella. "Let's make 'em swim home with their *shoes* on. That's the *pirate's* way. That's what Captain Flashpowder would do!"

"Captain ... Flashpowder?" repeated the cap'n. "You know Captain Flashpowder?"

Stitch Head's eye glinted in the midday sun.

"Do – do you?" he replied.

"Of course! It be my favourite storybook!" cried the cap'n. "Why, it's the book that made me want to be a sea captain. I've read it a hundred times!"

"Storybook…?" whispered Stitch Head, climbing down the crates to the deck.

"Aye! To adventure, and all that! See, you can't make me walk the plank! We have so much in common!" continued the cap'n hopefully. He reached into his coat and rooted around. "Truth be told, I still take it everywhere with me!"

Stitch Head watched in amazement as the cap'n pulled a book out of his coat pocket. It was battered and torn, but he recognized it immediately.

It was *The Daring Diary of Captain Flashpowder.*

ONWARD

(The truth about Captain Flashpowder)

"*Adventure is in the eye of the beholder.*"

From
*The Daring Diary of
Captain Flashpowder*

"I-I don't understand," whispered Stitch Head, staring at the book in the cap'n's hand. "Captain Flashpowder's diary … it's still in Castle Grotteskew. How could you have it?"

"There wasn't a boy in my town who didn't have a copy of *The Daring Diary of Captain Flashpowder* – but no one loved it as much as me, by criminy!" continued the cap'n. "So, does this mean we be friends now? Book buddies! You wouldn't make a Flashpowder fan walk the plank, would you?"

As Stitch Head peered at the cap'n's book, the truth slowly dawned on him. *The Daring Diary of Captain Flashpowder* wasn't a diary at all. It was a storybook. It was *all* just a story. He felt his borrowed blood run cold.

"But that means…" he murmured, holding his tiny hand up to his pirate's eye. "Flashpowder's not real?"

"I wish he were, by criminy! The world would be a more exciting place," replied the cap'n. "Still, we can always imagine, can't we?"

"Ha! You thought you were part pirate? Part *Flashpowder*?" Freakfinder laughed. "Lugs and mumbles, what a joke!"

"Shut your cake-hole, hog-face!" growled Arabella. "Unless you want Pox to eat your moustache!"

Stitch Head pulled the eyepatch off his head. Freakfinder was right. If Captain Flashpowder wasn't real, then his remarkable, ice-blue eye was just an eye.

"I'm – I'm not a pirate..." he whispered. "I'm not even *part* pirate."

"Oh, Stitch Head..." said the Creature. "I was so SURE."

Stitch Head slumped on to the deck. He felt as if he'd been tricked. Or perhaps, he had just seen what he wanted to see. Perhaps he had been fooling himself all along.

"That don't mean nothing!" shouted Arabella, scrabbling down from the crates. "Eye or no eye, you built a ship and set sail! You drew your sword and took over this whole ship *and* saved that reptile-faced master of yours! I ain't never seen more pirate-like behaviour in all my days! I don't care whose eyes you got, Stitch Head — ain't no one can take away what you *did*."

Stitch Head slowly looked up. He cast both eyes out to the shimmering ocean. It still looked as glorious as it did when he first put on the eyepatch and saw the world of adventure in his imagination. He may not have been part pirate, but Arabella was right. Something had changed. *He* had changed.

"The professor belongs in Castle Grotteskew. He always will," said Stitch Head. He turned to the cap'n. "If we let you go, will you take us back to the harbour, please?"

"Aye aye! Whatever you say," replied the cap'n. Then he pointed to Freakfinder. "And what about him?"

"Make him walk the plank!" snapped Arabella. "See how *he* likes swimming with the fishes!"

"Do your worst!" hissed a defiant Freakfinder. "I'm not scared of no *freaks*."

Stitch Head stared at Freakfinder.

"Let him go, too," he said finally. "If he's brave enough to go anywhere near Castle Grotteskew again, I'll be waiting for him."

"We'll *all* be waiting – boots at the ready!" growled Arabella. Then she turned to Stitch Head. "But ... do you *really* want to go back, Stitch Head? The professor might belong in the castle, but what about you?"

"YEAH, what about our GREAT ADVENTURE?" said the Creature.

"YaBBiT!" yapped Pox in agreement.

"I think I've had enough adventure for today," replied Stitch Head. He looked out to sea.

"But there's always tomorrow."

VISIT THE AUTHOR'S WEBSITE AT:

www.guybass.com

STRIPES PUBLISHING
An imprint of the Little Tiger Group
1 The Coda Centre, 189 Munster Road,
London SW6 6AW

A paperback original
First published in Great Britain in 2012

Text copyright © Guy Bass, 2012
Illustrations copyright © Pete Williamson, 2012

ISBN: 978-1-84715-228-2

Printed and bound in the UK.

6 8 10 9 7